The Epic of Mr. Poochikins vol. 1: Containing Chaos with A Padlock

AND OTHER POEMS

This book is a work of fiction. All characters, places, and events are of the author's imagination. Any similarities to real persons, living or dead, are coincidental.

This book was originally published in Minnesota, USA and is fully protected by copyright under the terms of the Library of Congress.

Copyright © 2021 Daft Media LLC. All rights reserved. Printed in the United States of America. No part of this book may be used without written permission except in the case of brief quotations in critical articles and reviews, or for educational purposes in an academic setting.

For information please email daftmedia@protonmail.com

ISBN 979-8-9897628-1-1

Dedication

Mom—

For putting up with all the Chaos as well as you ware able to while you were alive. RIP 03-15-2016. I hope you are with Jesus. You were praying again towards the end.

Courtney and Jak—

For putting up with my shit, lack of knowledge, lack of patience and lack of awkwardness, and also the random 2:00 A.M. texts. Please forgive me, sometimes I think I am a genius.

To anybody else—

You know if I either love you or hate you. So either fuck off or fuck off and die. [insert the heart emoji of your choice here]. <3

Seriously though, take the hint. If I am not talking to you and/or walking away from you, take THE HINT.

Table of Contents

	Page
The End of the Beginning is the Beginning of the End	2
Nana-nana, Boo-boo	4
Stain	6
Dread	7
Horizons	10
Strays	11
Leap	12
Butterflies	14
Right Now	18
Conflagration	20
Atoms of Hate	21
Unchambered (About School Shootings)	23
Pages	26
Pipelines	27
Rend to Mend	28

Wresting Will	29
Minnesota Winter	32
Bleaching Bones	33
Six Deep	34
My Last Laugh	35
Canto 0: The Parthenogenesis of Chaos and Creation of Time	37
Canto 1: Mr. Poochikins' Hiraeth	41
Canto 2: Mr. Poochikins' Smile	53
Canto 3: Mr. Poochikins' Temper	71

The End of the Beginning is the Beginning of the End

There's a chaos sphere moral compass
spinning like a bipolar clock,
twisting in pins,
letting tumblers
knock   -   knock
notching in brackets,
unlocking padlocks,
straight jackets,
and all the Gordian knots.

Count your blessings
down to

one.

Breaking chain links
    clink
        -clink
through the streets
around rampant-run
asylum feet. Pitter   patter
snickers sc   tt
       a   er.

Un shackled
laughter swarms
like a t r a m p l i n g
        herd
r e l e a s e d.

Unleash the black hΩle
Chaos
    singularity.

Scratch a new script.
Offset the balance
till the zeros and ones
reach negativity.
Blank-slate the lot.
Push the reset button
back to primordial
paradox | xodarap,

Nana-nana, Boo-boo

MY world's better than your world.
My world makes sense to me.
In my world I'm accepted.
In your world I'm a **FREAK**.

But my world is growing **bigger.**

It's **sssswelling**, splitting seams,

pulsating with a **throbbing** like a marching army's feet.

In my world, I am KING.

My world s p r e a d s its **fingers**
s t r e t c h i n g   o u t **to**

squeeze.

My hand opens its starving mouth,
saliva

ss
   p ii
       ll ll
         ii
           n
          g

            as it kneads.

In **my** world I'm a **GOD.**

Your world **IS** getting smaller,
blood wringing out like ink.

I slurp and lap it up
then let my imagination bleed.

In **your** world
I AM... u n l e a s h e d.

Stain

Black muck
coughed up–
hellfire pitch.
A drop-out,
waste pile,
clump of black shit-
stain on Society's skivvies,
a smiling Mark of Cain,
indelible and piling
always to remain,
fouling up the air,
take a whiff of my stank.
I'm firing from the helm
of a mega-ton tank.
I drip down,
seep in,
dig my way in.
A sprawling catalyst-pillar,
with a butterfly-grin.

Dread

Its
slither-
slick
fingers
sow
sour
notes
along
a
chalkboard
spine
with
a
scrap
metal
bow.
The
swan-song
hacksaws,
severs
with
a
screech,
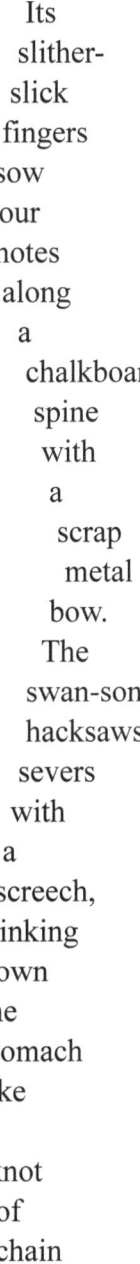
sinking
down
the
stomach
like
a
knot
of
chain
links.

AIR

Horizons

I
can never seem to see—
blind
from what's real and what's a dream.
Time, it's been so long inside these mental binds.
Prying at the stones that wall me as I rise,
reaching for the top in vain back to a crawl.
Bloody finger tips paint trails down as I fall.

Walls
never let me out.
Crawling,
I slowly writhe about.
Time stands me still,
my hands wish to rewind.
A rat without a race—
no reason to move on.
I close my eyes,
escape into my mind.
Alone,
outcast by a world where I don't belong.

All my horizons
have been broadened by lies.
I can't see past the dreams.
I can't see past reality.

Have I convinced myself a lie,
or is this the truth?
Have I a grip onto reality,
or have I let it loose?

Strays

Sleeping-dog lies with rabid bites.
A curled-up entangled mess.
Two lovers over, fight—
which one's the corpse?
which one's the carcass?

Her beauty's a beast with style.
Behind an innocent grin
she hides rose thorn razor wire,
waiting for the time to feed again.

Now feral from rejection,
my lips switchblade to knives,
hungry for reciprocation,
and I can't wait for the kiss goodbye.

We shattered our hearts and smiles,
glass turned back to sand.
Picked them up for another trial,
only to watch the grains slip from our hands.

From that Graceless apex,
cast to the wind's caress,
torn from our sides now as strays.

Flat backed, air knocked from chests.
One's sole on one's soul twists.
Forgiveness might come… but not today.

Leap

I take a leap of faith.
Now, I'm finally looking up.
Butterflies without wings
squirm in the pit of my guts.

Straight ahead is a sunny sky
and all the beauty I'm leaving behind.
I'm going to watch it all until the end
as I advance through my descent.

I'm not trying to leave a mark;
I'm just trying to leave.
I'm not trying to fly away;
I have no use for wings.
I'm told this is not the way,
but I don't feel the wind resisting me.

Death is an inevitability.
Life is a pending tragedy.
I lost it all before I took this fall.
Now, all that's before me is a curtain call.

My time is too sacrosanct for prayers.
Absolution lacks my want and care.
Not wasting thoughts on Salvation's grace,
there will soon be nothing left to save.

Chalk lines are in the post
of an empty silhouette.
As above, as so below,
as I lay me down to death.

I change my mind to close my eyes.
Still, I see it all drifting away.
I don't scream and I don't cry,
I simply hit the pave…

Butterflies

I'm not done with killing myself inside.
I keep chasing butterflies.

I can't knead the need away.
No senses sensing sense for change.
Postmortem states
living's too late.
X'd out eyes
pattern my decay.

Sick of myself,
not sick of my hell—
living for new ways to die.

Necropsy reports that I'm no corpse,
but death breaches its leeching hands,
gently stroking as we dance,
no strangers to this romance.
Peel back the hides that bind,
inject him directly into my bloodline.

Tension rising
anticipation
needing sedation.
Cobweb-cogwheels
counter clockwise,
turn my cognition.

Sick of myself,
not sick of my hell—
living for new ways to die.
I'll coddle myself
from the World—it's not well—

and kill myself till I'm alive.

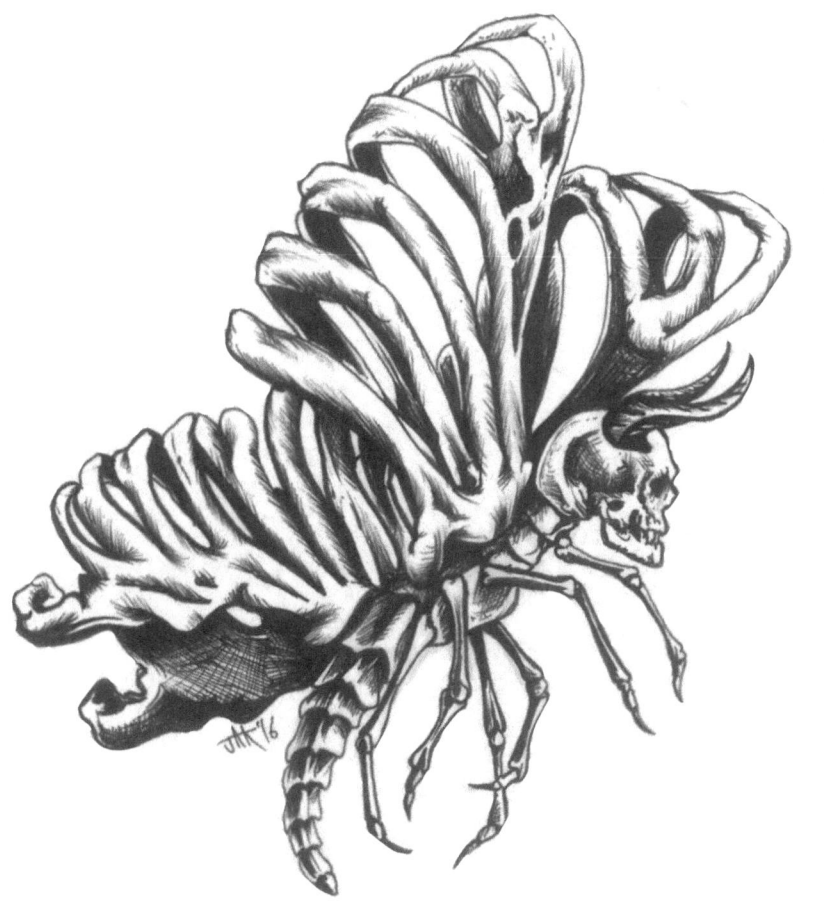

16

FIRE

17

Right Now

I feel like razing the Earth
and eating its ash
like some feeble-minded dragon
with a severe mineral deficiency
and a bad case of pica.

Because the right people aren't suffering here.
Because I thought…

Right now,
I got an itch a canyon's smile wide,
and as deep as a bottomless cave dive,
and like a madhouse mad-case of bad crabs
it's gnawing at my insides
like some cracked-out cannibals
in an I eating contest.

And so,
here I am
once again,
left and betrayed,
soaking in a bloodbath of hindsight.

How I wish the World would burn,
right now.
Then, I would know
you're burning with me too

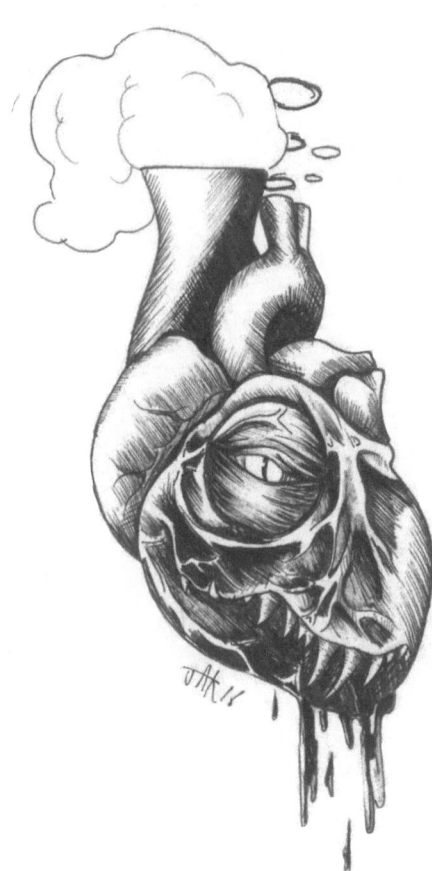

Conflagration

Charring fires
tongue out a beast.
Snap-lapping mouth
regurgitates and eats.
Spewing out
from its cusp
cums the basest lusts,
I'm soon spent and
fatigued.

A coal machine churns,
thickening
potash and peat
fumes bellowing
brimstone halos,
smoking rings.
My heart beats
cardiac disease.

As septic excess
drips from her
Sunday best
to prettify her pink,
ravage, leave, repeat.

This is how her blood
flows.
Where her veins grow—
don't know—where her
heart is
but I know that it doesn't
beat.

Atoms of Hate

A few synapses short.
A few circuits break.
My judgment distorts.
My pretty face reanimates.

My mind is a battlefield.
My brain is under war.
I'm having complications
holding up the frontal fore.
There's Chaos all around.
There's nowhere to run, no safe ground.

Cellular separation.
Chemicals not synchronized.
Cerebral aberration.
Atoms split, I divide.
Shining black rage
blinding me with hostility.
Atoms of hate
deteriorated any sense
I've left to make.

I'm not hearing reason.
I shall not rationalize.
Sometimes there is no ear for
putting differences aside.
Basics of human nature:
We all have our bitter sides.
And the only thing that makes sense now
is that you have to die.

Unchambered (About School Shootings)

I'm a seething steam-engine,
and War is a big, mad monkey at the helm
hanging on the whistle like he's swinging from a jungle vine.
A shovel in his hand is a battle ax
hacking off heaps of my coal-heart, stoking it in a stove
until it's glowing like a fiend's smile puffing out smoke.
I wore a mask made of storm-calm
until lucidity left, came back knocked up and gave birth to
this lunatic.
The quacks at the clinics with their chicken-scratch talk
couldn't lift a mental fingerprint if it was on a planted glove.
All masks off, expose my Halloween-grimace.
I'm headed straight toward a Grimm make-believe finish.
My eyes smile wide as my thumb cocks

the machine whose steel will be seizing ticktocks,
swissin' up skin with a spray of its kin
in a kettledrum rat-a-tat,
spitting out the mouth of a beast of a barrel
like an angel's trumpet shoutin' out
megatons of C-4 off like a world war.
Those steel beasts unchambered are unhitched and now pissed
and coming around the bend each the circumference of a fist.
There's gonna be blood.
Oh, there's gonna be raging,
and no one will live long enough to murmur
'save me'.

✓ WATER

Pages

As I so painfully
flip through these pages, these memories.
I open, the seams rip.
I can't keep these binds stitched.
It's like a spiral down the drain
counterclockwise against the grain—
soaking in a bath of glass,
thumbing through thoughts of the past.

I can't keep my head straight.
I've tried everything but fucking tape.
I'm undone,
the ends are f r a y e d,
wearing me down
string
by
string,
wrapping me
in my tomb.
I blossom
into a swoon.
All these pages,
these memories
mark the start of my
unraveling.

Pipelines

Barbed wire heartbeat
not malleable to flatline.
Wrought iron rose thorns.
Black tar pipelines.
Serpentine teeth digging,
hypodermic knives skinnin'.
Gotta suckle from the snake's bite
to spit out the venom.

Pick your poison,
prick in your plaque.
It all comes wrapped in cellophane.
Sweat it out,
bleed it back in,
the spiral takes you further in.
Pick your corpse up,
up and run,
follow track marks with open arms.
Sweat it out,
bleed it back in,
the spiral takes you down again.

Rend to Mend

I'm dirty,
filthy,
tainted with impurities.
My body is rotting
so amputate the limbs diseased.
Cut off the infections.
Cure me with some injections.
Fix me with lacerations.
Let me of these impurifications.

Drain me clean.
Let me bleed and bleed.
Drain me clean.
Let me.

My heart pumps with filth
I'm so sick. I'm so ill.
I see me decay.
I see me wilt.

Split the skin.
Spill me open.
The cuts will cleanse.
I gotta rend to mend.

Let me.

Wresting Will

Standing in the center of a fold
of a chapter collapsing.
Cold sweat washes away the calm.
My train of thought jack-knifes.

Reflections scar as they seam,
The glaring past looking through me 20/20.
Tilting my head to six,
I turned to seven nixed
enduring these
reflections shattering me.

I am the glass that's looking back.
My attempts to smile cause me to crack
as I break back
into dirt.
Regret charges me like a beast
and is devouring
my heart
lives only from these beatings.

Stale breath empties the chest.
I collapse with my lungs,
then fill back in with an air of fresh regrets.
Nothing heals, nothing betters, nothing grows,
now only Nothing's left.

Reflections scar as I scream.
Shards of the past ripping through me bloody, bloody.
Stripping the flesh, trying to find
the child, the boy from another time,
still born yet razed by
the hands that birthed the beast.

31

EARTH

Minnesota Winter

I never felt its cold
until it gravely crept across my plot.
The sky sifts a snow that folds
into death bed clots.

A scoliosis embrace grows
shivers up a glass spine.
Nerves branching out for hope
wither frozen, out of line.

My crippling limbs devour
like a wilting flower
whose once sweet beauty
has since ripened soured.

I crack. It cuts.
As disembodied blood gushes
a corrupted cookie cut through
with veins of red-winged roads
mapping out their bends,
where nothing grows
and everything ends.

Bleaching Bones

Closeted skelesins sewn
in this Broken Home's grain,
hidden in the bones,
keyed-in deep and stained.

I taste-test to excess
with cesspit-lips,
sucking sin from fleshpots
with gargantuan sips.

Reaching new lows
just to crawl home
where my body macerates
in the dross of sin.
No gods will now forgive,
I've gotta cheat to win
by tearing down my temple
to only catacombs,
ripping off the past
then bleaching these bones.

My mouth's a full-metal jacket,
lying in this world of shit.
Squeezing off silver-tongue spit,
leaving,
smiling
exit wound pits.

Six Deep

Beneath.
Confined.
Coffin nails shut you inside.
Buried alive,
clawing at satin and pine.
All your screams
won't save you by any means,
not a peep,
not when you're six deep.

As you plead,
writhing in a six by three—
hail a prayer—
your steepled hands will hold nothing there,
then collapse underneath
a ton of earth and the soul it keeps.

Stripped down to bone,
you're all alone,
naked in the dark you call home,
I saw past your pose.
You've been exposed,
now only your true colors show,
and they're not silver and gold.

Blame yourself.
You've dug your own hell.
You've no worth.
You're just dirt.
You're just dirt.
Dead earth.

My Last Laugh

After death,
after life,
before the afterlife lie
doesn't come with Shangri-La
and it's shiny white lights.

After bones,
after ashes,
after dust…
When the wind whistles low
with a dirge of its gusts,
I'll be there
smiling
with a mouth of straight blades
and a razor-strop tongue.
My big bear trap yap's
gonna be Ha! Ha! hacking up your faces
with the guttural quakes
from its seismic laugh.

Canto 0:
The Parthenogenesis of Chaos and Creation of Time

In a paradox place of a time without Time.
Before spacial form fixed, first, Chaos was prime.
A serpentine beast that as its skin shed and molted,
seeded and reaped life as it folded and unfolded.
Purging offspring from its black womb abyss,
it would devour them back into complete nothingness.
From cold and stagnant to boiling and roiling,
this twisting dark mass kept coiling and uncoiling.
No glimmer of light shone from it ever,
not until her young rose up against her.
    Of them, twelve had cunning enough to survive
and stay alive, escaping her cannibalistic filicide.
In the dark, they gathered to plot an upheaval
against their parent, the Most Ancient Primeval.
The eldest of them, established a plan:
To encircle the beast, then await his command.
    When birthing, their parent retracted in size,
giving enough time to enact the plan they devised.

He dispatched his attack, so to all rest,
one after the other, till she was suppressed.
From there they shaped and bent down the beast,
forging an Order within this belt of brutality.
Chaos was without light, they illuminated it;
Chaos was without height, they rose above it;
Chaos was without weight, they grounded it;
Chaos was without form, they contained it.
    Quelled but not killed, they kept Chaos confined,
as it knew no end or concept of Time.
Within a box of dust and spacial debris,
the Twelve caged her away with no lock or key.
Instead they formed a lid, a disc to encase,
called it earth, then laid it on top like a grave.
As the earth dried, it cracked into canyons and ravines,
so they filled those veins with water, making rivers and seas.
Oceans soon grew and with them came the breeze.
And above them all: light, to feed all of their needs.
    Balance would be needed to maintain their Order,
so they established a council to form limits and borders.
The next thing they created was Time's existence,
as past, present and future occurred within the same instance.
The length of their battle and the attacks therein
would calendar their year and the months within.
To signify their triumph over Chaos' watch,
their religion would be symbolized with a clock.
A reminder so that no one forgot
a life before Order, before Chaos was fought.
Twelve Godheads, twelve months, so twelve hours to a clock.
without these numbers all time would stop.
    However, the Twelve knew there would come a day
when the beast would be freed and Chaos would reign.
Because in that pit beneath the ground—that basement of dirt—
Chaos stewed, and its anger festered the longer it lurked.

End Canto 0

Canto 1:
Mr Poochikins' Hiraeth

    Mr Poochikins woke from the same dream
he's had since his consciousness came into being.
He jolted up, reached out to grasp
hard onto something as if falling fast.
Then a searing feeling of singeing skin synced
with the falling sensation while his stomach sinked
like a hot-pan of panicking butterflies
cut through his stomach with razor sharp knives.
    He could never recall what the nightmare was—
just vague feeling of amnesiac fuzz,
of a deja vu puzzle where illusions ceased
then faded into images that could not be pieced.
A melancholic longing for a home never known
with a phantom-limb feeling for someone unknown.

And then a wistful smile kissed his lips
as there was always a small passing of happiness
afterward that got him out for the day's mien
as he rolled out of bed, with content—his machine.
    Considered base-born by ones called the Wight,
they dressed him in clothes with black and white stripes.
This was the way in which he was condemned,
barred from ever being accepted by them.
    He lived in the Chrysalis of Concrete and Tin,
but stayed on the Squaller Side far deep within.
If one walked the rim of the Chrysalis compound,
three weeks worth of paces wouldn't take one around.
The walls of the Chrysalis were mountain crag's high,
towering stories halfway to the sky.
They kept the creatures of the Forest Melina out,
while ejecting black waste from its sewage-spouts.
    The Wight housed him in the Place of Unwanted Things,
which they had dubbed *The House of Poochikins*.
He called for no visitors, and received no requests,
as he had no friends to ever make guests.
Even his memories had left him astray
as he knows no knowledge of his past to this day.
The closest he's known of a motherly womb
was the cot where he laid in this concrete cocoon.
    And since that day his consciousness came into effect,
Mr. Poochikins' known Torment's caress.
By brutal beatings and bludgeoning rites,
by gluts of his blood had he been baptized.
His spirit was bound to his bones and his flesh,
fraternal twins in a dyadic mesh,
so each time his body crossed the hand of abuse,
his cognitive engine became damaged and bruised.
    He was misread like an upside-down book—
an unwanted read based off of its looks.

His hair was absent of pigment and dye,
which accented the yellow in his saddened eyes.

The length his left leg was longer in length
than his right which gave him a limp to his gait.
    The Wight thought of him as quite odd,
not normal, bizarre, freakish and flawed.
But normal, to him, was a relative concept
based on the backgrounds of personal precepts.
He thought: *The odd might be strange, the odd might be weird,
but weird is not weird unless normal is near.*
Tired of the same old sites, the same old sounds,
the same same-old way the same-old was wound,
he often guised under the veil of a hood
concealing the familiar way that he looked,

he wondered the walkways of the Chrysalis,
avoiding the Wight, their eyes and their limbs.

Hunched over like one in a cold, windy winter,
hesitant like a boy avoiding a splinter,
he kept his eyes downcast, while the walkways to him
looked like an unreal reel of celluloid film.
Life seemed so fictitious, things always amiss,
something was absent from inside Mr. Poochikins,
like a piece was cookie-cut right from his guts,
in gingerbread-man fashion, eyes glazed with wanderlust.
    One day, while tucked in a day-dreamy sense
a screech tore away the Air's blanket of silence,
revealing a massive, black, cast-iron beast,

known as the Iron Horse, bellowing out steam.
The crooked spine of the tracks that it traveled
snaked down to the Chrysalis' sub-levels,
where many vainly mined in darkness for gold
but always ended digging up only coal.
And as the mercantile vessel traveled below,
the Monolith's bells chimed then ignited its Glow.
    As punishment for the Wights' lack of worship
the Godheads denied natural light from the Chrysalis.
So the Mayor King, being an inventive one,
placed on the Monolith an artificial Sun.
The Monolith stood like a stone cataract
poured from the sky then froze completely intact.
Like a case of stairs but without its steps,
scaling up to the Celestial Ocean unchecked.
The base of which ended in the Chrysalis' center,
resembling a sundial the way both were structured.
After the bells chimed, the Glow shined away
but only a dull and doleful dim gray.
    Now high up the Monolith, on a balustraded stage,
the Mayor King stood and dictated his ways.
With a megaphone-voice he ministered all moral beliefs
for the Wight and anyone who gave him their knee.
Hearing too much, Mr. Poochikins moved on his way,
but the Monolith is where his attention was paid.
This action of negligence came with great cost
as his path and someone else's had crossed.
A women with a face like dead bark on a tree
with a cold, steely glare, so cold it could freeze
and it did as Mr. Poochikins' jaw sagged
when he realized it was the Red Eyed Hag.
    The Hag was the matron to him and the Wight.
She counseled the thoughts of the Mayor-King's mind,
filling his ears with her wisdom and whispers,
while whipping the Wight into shape with her orders.

She stood there, snarling at him, looking harried,
as he caused her to drop all the objects she'd carried.
Quickly dropping down, he began to gather
everything up, but to her this didn't matter.
Like a chain to a slave, bad times were bound to his leg,
dragging behind wherever he walked with his lame.
The length of her cane met cross with his face,
mixing black and blue hues into lattice lace shapes.
She beat him so hard she split open his skull.
He fell to the ground like a dropped rag doll.
His position went fetal, kissing forehead to knees,
protecting the most vital parts from her beatings.
As her limbs lashed out, so did her tongue,
and just like her limbs, it viciously swung:
    "You malformed misfit, dumb, brutish mutant,
aberration from all that is decent.
Squeeze back in the twat of whatever whore bore you.
Save us the displeasure of looking upon you."
    Despite the abuse that occurred in his life
no salt ever shed from Mr. Poochikins' eyes.
All of those tears only welled up within,
never draining away, always therein.
As she beat him he shrank down in his size,
something that often occurred at these times.
While his brain sloshed around from shore to shore
damage occurred, back lobe to front fore.
And instead of his vision fading to black,
it sharply contrasted the opposite path,
as the Wight began to spread around him
blurring into one large body of pale skin.
Their pallid pallors pooled like liquid debris
and soon he was drowning in faceless sea.
    Numb in his mind and so numb to his senses,
he rose to his knees as Reason's edge kept bending.

As blood torrentially flowed down from his face,
his vision went red, then blackened with rage.
The gore dripped quickly, he chaliced his hands,
and it gathered thickly like hourglass-sands.

His mind reached back and pulled up the past,
an all too real reel-to-reel image began to cast:
Him being beaten with sticks, bloodied with bricks,
smeared with excrement and showered with piss.
Names that were called, every title a thorn,
brambles of stems where no pedals were born.

Then, piercing through the massive body of white,
two perfect red holes bit through like a spider's bite.
They grew bigger like wide rimmed glasses of wine,
drunk with a madness with no sobering signs.
Kneeling there he stayed still and motionless,
calm in poise until a great madness gripped.
Something occurred inside him unknown,
every muscle in his body expanded with growth.
His eyes started to twitch, then their colors switched
from deep sulfurous yellow to a mercurial pitch.
His temper flared up. His eyes began to glow.
Then the air around him both scalded and froze.
Feeling weak he breathed, which gave into heaves,
then he noticed salvation lay down at his knees:
A rounded object like a lead-heavy pipe
but with a sweet scent and was spirally striped.
Then he heard the Hag creeping closer towards him,
which struck him with fear so he struck out before him.
A crack sounded out and silenced all sounds,
putting its fingers across the lips of all those around.
His vision started to clear and come back,
just in time to see the Hag's head whip viciously back.
A putrid cloud of rot and disgust,
spewed from her mouth as her teeth turned to dust.
She fell like a dirt clod filling a grave,
tripped over the tracks into the Iron Horse's way.
Black adamantine steel met with her flesh, made it bust,
then speckled the crowed in a muddied blood-gust.
  The Wight began to surround Mr. Poochikins,
closing the gap between them and him.
But before the length of the Iron Horse passed
Mr. Poochikins leapt on and held to it fast.
He sat on the train between relief and disbelief
as the train path continued he felt a cathartic release.

His fear leveled out and his body learned compromise,
shrinking back down while his welts retained their size.
Then he noticed he still had gripped in his hand
the object that saved him from Hag's reprimands.
It was a candy cane, gigantically cast,
large enough to hold the weight of one man.
Wiping the blood from the crook of the cane,
he palmed it to even the limp of his leg,
then proudly roamed 'round the mercantile train
as they traveled together along the same way.
　　He stowed away near the head of the iron beast,
and decided to hide until he could properly think.
But something entranced him about the cane,
a feeling deep down that he couldn't explain.
He was spellbound and not just by its sight,
it's sweet smell is what really weakened his mind.
Without thinking he bit down onto the cane
and a war between his teeth and it came.
He shattered it and out scattered debris,
turning the large cane into an amputee.
Saliva and thick, gooey candy cane drool
ran down his chin into fluorescent pools.
His hands were caked with sugar and dye,
so he licked them clean until his tongue went dry.
His insides felt funny, so he held out his head
of the nearest window and leaned over its ledge.
His stomach flipped between rapture and blight,
at one point he felt such euphoric delights,
then hundreds of butterflies totting sharp knives
flew around eviscerating his insides.
Strange things he'd never seen once in his life
started to stir around inside his sights.
Shadows unhinged themselves from their settled spots,
as the Glow of the Monolith grew legs and ran off.

He stood for a spell, gearing up his thinks,
toying with his hands, trying to make sense of things.
The celluloid walkways rolled up into reels.
Suddenly, he forgot how to breathe and to feel.
He then became so overwhelmingly possessed by fatigue,
more so than he ever thought possible to achieve.
So he laid his head down upon an iron frame
and slipped into a sleep that would last for days.

End Canto 1

51

Canto 2:
Mr. Poochikins' Smile

   Mr. Poochikins woke up to a new day,
not from the ting-tong-tang that the Monolith rang,
but from an intolerable throbbing,
gravely pulsating from his speak-cave.
Blood from his heart punched his jaw as it pumped
a thah-thump-thump beat as the oral pain drummed.
   "Curses!" He yelped, as he came to with a start.
"What is this pain ripping my mouth apart?"
   He sat up faster than a brain synapse snaps,
trying to wrap his mind around what happened last.
Then a jolting comment sent a shock through the air
from an ill-mannered voice in quite ill-repair:
   "And up pops the freakishly long legg'd deformity.
How's life outside the bell tower, Quasi?"
   He opened his eyes, but quickly closed them tight
as the light around him was blindingly bright.
     The man spoke again: "Need me to close the shades a bit?
You're squinting your face like you're taking a tough shit."
   Laughter roared from the man as he basked,
then was silenced by glugs from a half-empty flask.
Mr. Poochikins felt the ground shift about
as the man tromped and lumbered around.

As the blinding light diminished and dimmed,
a blessing of darkness surrounded him.
Then in the gloom, he faced the jeering waster
whose physical features could not be discerned.
And with every throb of his oral pain,
his vision's clarity waxed and waned.
   He decided to stand up, but once on his feet,
he discovered his muscles had all atrophied.
His limbs were the consistence of rubber and gel,
so when his legs gave out, he quickly fell.
His body poured out like a spill on the floor,
spanning out vainly in search of a container.
So he crawled around like a bum seeking change,
purchased some ground, but no balance was gained.
A wheezing cackle, a chuckle of sorts,
accompanied the slaps he palmed out on the floor.
This symphony of the sounds made a sorrowful sight,
as he slipped back and forth and side to side.
Finally, he compromised with logic and physics,
and positioned himself on the floorboards to sit.
   Time went by to help him collect his thoughts,
so that he could find out which ones were lost.
As his muddled mind cleared so too did his sight,
so he asked the man if he could shed some light.
Brightness ignited from an unblinded window,
exposing the harsh rays of the Monolith's Glow.
And in that flash, he remembered it all,
every glut of gore, every horror recalled:
The Red-Eyed Hag had met her demise,
and Mr. Poochikins was the reason she died.
   His mind now kept getting wound up in knots
until they all tangled around the same thoughts:
Have I been imprisoned? Have I been caught?
Had Time come instead for me to pay up the cost?
Breaking from this mental state, he finally asked,

"Are you a jailer? Has some sentenced been passed?"
   He received his question's answer
in the guise of bellowing laughter.
And with it, a rank stench so foul arose
sending Mr. Poochikins back down in repose.
   "Your breath," he said while covering his nose,
"Smells like your teeth have completely decomposed."
   "HA!" the man burst, "Your teeth look worse than mine stink.
Here, grab hold of this looking glass and take a peek."
His hand waved wildly until his grasp caught handle
upon a reflection that was even harder to handle.
Mr. Poochikins brought the object nearer
until he faced the end joke of a funhouse mirror.
Staring back at him from the glassy pool
was the countenance of a man gone a fool.
What he noticed first was his left eye
now had a polished and silvery shine.
The right was the same sulphuric gold,
and unlike the former, seemed in control.
   The pain from his mouth dug its pins in again
which spurred up the urge to wince a crude grin.
Cracking open his mouth he peered into pure horror.
His jaw dropped in shock—a frame of mouth sores—
a cavernous pit of stalactites and stalagmites,
like a halo of conical graves inside a burial site.
The cane he ate left its violent, candied wrath,
as his teeth were now an after meth aftermath.
   He directed his gaze up and caught a new sight
of a great fat man most unlike the Wight.
The man was thickset and astoundingly stocky,
and his skin color was like thick teriyaki.
His chest and belly were one round solid mass,
like he'd consumed a 60-gallon wine cask.
His hair was pulled back, cropped up in rows,
frosted with age like light snow on a tarred road.

5

5

Hanging, tied up to his long beard was a flask,
one made of fine glass with a timepiece attached.
Suspenders strapped up his overall-pants,
with smears coal soot smudged down the expanse.
   On seeing this man in his torn-up condition
Mr. Poochikins knew that he was in no prison.
So he quickly sprang up from the ground to leave,
but his mind and body were still very weak.
In a swoon, he surveyed his surroundings and swayed
like a dangling man who'd been noosed up and hanged.
Other than liquor bottles, either emptied or rationed,
altars of clocks riddled the room, religiously fashioned.
   "Exactly who are you? A zealot lush?" He said snidely.
"Or a faith-starved derelict bartering drinks for dignity?"
   "Take it easy, Pooch. I's just foolin'.
Don't go throwing me in front'a train too."
   The heavily built, black man laughed as he spoke,
holding his hands up in a feigned defensive pose.
He then sighed after taking a disappointing sip,
then let these words spill out from his liquor-less lips:
   "The Mayor King put a bounty on your head:
Dead or alive but preferably dead.
Don't worry, he thinks you got off at the last station,
that you blindsided me and are at some other location."
   Mr. Poochikins thought about something he'd learned:
No one does something without wanting something in return.
   "Well, then who are you, if not like the Wight?
And why is your skin painted as black as night?
What's your end game? Why are you helping me?"
he questioned, with a scorching air of scrutiny.
   "HaHA! Thaz good. Thaz real good, mehn.
My skin ain't painted. Been n'is color since 'fore Time began.
And you don't owe me nuthin', mehn.
I just trying to lend a helping hand.

Seven straight days have now elapsed
since I found you locked in that mental lapse.
I tried, in vein, many times to waken you,
but that wasn't something you were taking to.
So I moved you to my own personal train car."
Then the man walked over to a stocked liquor bar.

 Puzzled to pieces, Mr. Poochikins nervously laughed,
before telling himself to calm down and ask:

 "Train car? Seven days? Wha… What are you saying?
Are we on the Iron Horse? Why isn't it moving?"

 "What? You think I eat, sleep and shit this thing?
I'm on my break. Work'll wait 'till I'm done with my drink."

 "But… you're the one that's supposed to keep this train tracked.
You're the engineer, and you're completely smashed."

"YUUUUP! I conduct and keep the sexy beast a'chuggin'."
He said, pausing again as his flask started glugging.
Then offered Mr. Poochikins to shake his hand
and said "And My name is Nick. Nick Knave, mehn."
Mr. Poochikins returned the gesture and simply stated:
"You. Are so. Intoxicated."
What light cracking through the window screens
showed shadows being unsown from their casted seams,
inching down like black streams of wet ink
spilled on a canvas for Gravity to drink.
They dangled like strings then stitched up and linked
tautly to Mr. Poochikins pulling him up as they synched.
He felt removed from himself then felt urged to leave.
As his body moved forward his mind took a backseat.
"I have to go." Mr. Poochikins said in a monotonous tone,
then walked to the door like a sleepwalking drone.
"You got cobwebs clogging up your cogwheels?"
Nick asked. "Leavin' right now in't exactly ideal.
If I's you, I wouldn't be showin' my face at all,
since turning the Red-Eyed Hag into a red-eyed rag doll."
"I really don't have time for your prattling on.
Find other ears for this sowing-circle talk to fall upon,"
Mr. Poochikins snapped back, concluding their talk.
Then he opened the door, compelled to go walk.
Dazed in the day, he dizzily trekked the walkways,
guided by the shadows attached to his arms and legs.
Oddly enough, no Wight shared the streets then,
yet he felt like someone was walking with him.
Eventually, he came to a colossal marquee
of giant white teeth, smiling eerily,
announcing loudly, "DENTAL PRACTITIONER,"
then whispering softly, "self-proclaimed puppeteer."
The last title seemed deterring and daunting,
but his teeth were in pain, and the big sign was calling.

As Mr. Poochikins passed through the entrance,
light from outside made the dark inside present.
His thoughts went rampant, tripping as they ran,
while shadows danced wildly without a master's hands.

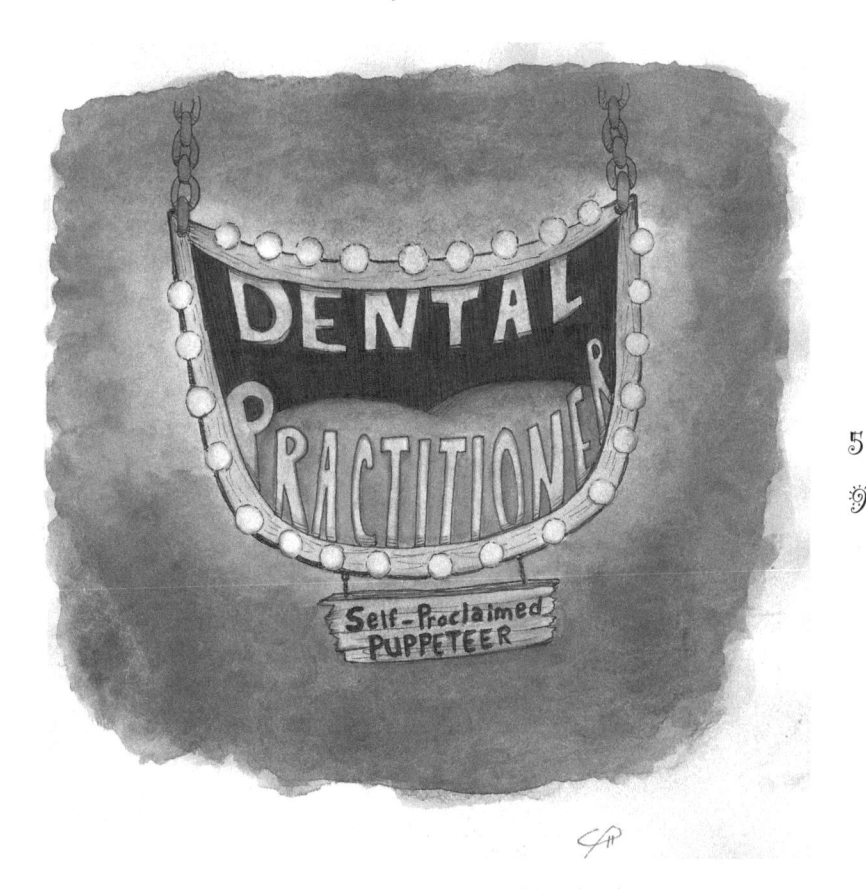

Always in his peripheral were thin bodily shades,
but when spied upon them they would shy away.
A pungent aroma, with a sharp, stuck sneeze burn,
spilled out through the doors as he inhaled it in.
Jars of dark fluid were stacked upon shelves,
and walled along the shop the deeper he delved.
    "More foulness," he expressed as he gagged and retched.
"Who would keep stock of something so easy to detest?"

"The miasma you smell," said a voice crawling from the back,
"is condensed mist from the Celestial Ocean's black."
　　A man standing next to a dental chair, clowned
with a 10-mile wide smile that never shrank down,
said: "Hi. Come inside. Sit down, Mr. Poochikins.
I've been expecting you since my doors opened."
　　He was scrubbed up in a bleach-white latex gown,
starched so stiff it would break if it fell to the ground.
Light from his slick hair shined from fresh wax,
and his eyes gleamed as if they were looking at a snack.
The skin of his face had a sinister stretch
and was tightly latched back towards his face-line's hedge,
where metal hooks wound around like a serpentine
grounded on his skin like a neoprene mask fit for Halloween.
His smile never leveled from its constant grin.
If there were a Devil then this would be his twin.
But still, he had charm, a bit of magnetism,
drawing in Mr. Poochikins despite his suspicions.
His attitude was convincing and quite professional,
enough to make a priest spill their hearts in a confessional.
　"How can you stomach such an odious odor?"
Mr. Poochikins asked, expecting an answer.
　　"So quick to question… So quick to question,
but never really learning a lesson."
The doctor-man said, then with a dramatic flair
invited Mr. Poochikins again to sit in his chair.
He was so compelled that he quickly did what was asked,
then the doctor wrapped an apron around his neck just as fast.
When Mr. Poochikins sat down, he knocked over a peculiar cane.
The doctor picked it up and nostalgically explained,
　　"This quackery instrument was used in bloodletting,
to rid people of sickness and disease, after some razoring.
The blood flows down, taking a helical path,
twisting into a wash basin made up of brass.

It has since not been used for some time,
but stained still from its now immoral crimes."
 "Thank you, good doctor, for that unsolicited fact,
but I need your help, could we get back on track?"

"A good doctor I may be, but Dr. Good, I am."
He said with and awkward and hyena-like laugh.
The doctor spun around, hunched over a tray,
put his hands up to his face, then ripped it away.
Mr. Poochikins noticed when he turned back around,
the doctor orphaned his smile and adopted a frown.

In an overly dramatic and theatrical pose
the doctor attentively sat as Mr. Poochikins spoke,
  "It feels like someone's bit into my teeth!
The pain's so severe. Do you think you could help me?"
So Dr. Good examined his patient's mouth,
poking, prodding and tapping around.
Mr. Poochikins writhed and kicked in his seat
but the sadist kept sticking and stabbing his teeth.
  "You have cavernous pits all up in your pearlies,
but I'll drill, fill and cap up all of those cavities.
I also specialize in prosthetic-tinks—
machinations and devices for abnormalities.
Do you have insurance or some way to pay?
Otherwise, I can credit you for the stay."
  "Insurance and credit. I've heard of those before.
Are they some sort of homeopathic-type cures?"
  Ignoring the question, turning around for a while,
the doctor spun back again with his game-show host smile.
  "Let's size your right leg up with a prosthetic,
and make that long left one seem less pathetic.
You should have braces. Your teeth got the crooks.
They'll straighten all the crannies and align all the nooks.
We'll put a new swing to your style, one more becoming.
My good man, I have the answers to all your short-comings.
With my prosthetic-tinks, and some meds for your thinks,
you'll finally be the one everyone expects you to **be**.
A nominal fee is all that's decreed,
but let's not put prices on health or beauty."
  "Well, you sure are," Mr. Poochikins said,
but still, he nodded and gave him the go-ahead.
  A long while went by before Mr. Poochikins left,
and when he did he had donned some new threads:
Thick iron wires and braces encompassed his head,
keeping his lips parted and creepily widespread,
He had a grin like half of a coin, but not one of joy,

more like a grimace of one severely annoyed.
His cavities and teeth had been fixed up at least;
however, great pain possessed his now un-crooked teeth.
Some rough leather patched-up the sight of his eye,
the one that turned tinny before the Hag's demise.
His leg supplements were bolted and latched
onto his thigh with a small engine attached.
A contraption that needed a kickstart.
A paradox, he thought, *for a prosthetic part.*
The brace on his leg had a stilt so unnecessarily high
that he needed a forearm crutch to keep his balance just right.
He limped and he lumbered like a 3-limbed spider,
one victimized by the whims of childhood torture.

  Crowds of the Wight were out and about.
He passed by them all and not one incident broke out.
They stared intently not recognizing who they saw,
only that someone was fixing their social flaws.
Someone was changing their abnormalities,
to the standard the Wight held themselves to be.

  His footsteps were loud, hydraulic and heavy,
sounding like a beastly piece of mobile machinery.
Plumes of black smoke billowed as the engine wailed,
creating a thick stream much like a chemical trail.
Though it was noisy and polluted the streets
oh, how the Wight accepted these things.
Several hamsters, which ran upon wheels,
made up the cogs in welded spoked steel.
The exhaust caused them and the hamsters to wheeze,
but how the Wight smiled, accepting these things.

  He was feeling unsure of how things had worked out,
and being accepted did not relinquish his doubts.
Feeling confused he decided to go home,
but once he arrived he saw the place was torn down.
He found only remains of scorched woodwork and stones,
resembling an animal burnt down to its bones.

6
4

He had nothing left, nothing of his own.
No place to belong, no place to call home.
He decided to walk back to the train,
and talk to the drunkard, Nick Knave.
And as he waded past more of the Wight
the Monolith chimed the last hour before night.
    The lights from inside the parked Iron Horse shined,
so Mr. Poochikins went up to it and knocked several times.
After a long while, Nick answered the door
but stopped short as his jaw hit the floor.
He looked at Mr. Poochikins in shock and revolt
but grinned devilishly as he jestingly spoke:
    "Mehn, you look like the Tin Man's bastard love-child
with the deformed daughter of a retarded scrap pile.
Did you lose a bet? Or smoke a bunch of crack?
Why would you ever wanna dress like that?"
    "Save it," Mr. Poochikins pleaded. "I got no place to go,
and all of those Wight bastards destroyed my home.
    "Well, get in then, you sorrowful being.
Since the Hag died, the night comes with dark things."
    So, Mr. Poochikins entered with that invitation,
just as the Monolith chimed the day's final din.
    The exhaust from Mr. Poochikins' prosthetic engine
smoked up the Iron Horse beyond comprehension,
so when he sat down he extinguished the fumes
lest they continued to pollute Nick's room.
As Mr. Poochikins let his leg-engine seize
the hamsters inside heaved a reprieve.
Nick noticed the little guys labored to breathe,
so he gave what water and food he had to eat.
    Mr. Poochikins noted Nick was still drinking,
and thought that by now his blood must be pure whiskey.
But his feet did not trip, nor did his words ever slur,
though the stench of him would make another man stagger.

Nick then settled down in front of Mr. Poochikins
who seemed more lost than when he had first left him.
He looked at the scrap-metal-man up and down,
then curtly spoke as he rose up one brow,
    "Now, tell me, why are you wearing all of that crap?
Have you gone into another mental lapse?"
    Mr. Poochikins paused after Nick's request
sighed, then frustratingly confessed:
    "I wanted to fit in with the Wight and clique.
Because I'm not happy with being myself, Nick.
I'm always rejected. I never belong.
And I don't understand how being me is wrong.
I did feel accepted when I walked with the Wight,
but something inside of me just doesn't feel right."
    A look more grave than gray on a grave
took over the jovial appearance of Nick's face.
With a nod of understanding, Nick sat in silence,
carefully choosing his words before giving this guidance:
    "I'm not sure if I'm the one to help you with this,
but one has to accept one's self to find happiness.
Posing and imposing a presence of who you are or not
is a fast-track way of finding out that you're lost.
Maybe you should turn up your direction,
and ask the Godheads for an explanation?"
    Mr. Poochikins scoffed in Nick's face
then verbally spat his hateful distaste:
    "I will not direct faith, nor put stock in belief,
into unseen faces with tricks up their sleeves.
They're bullies with power, no better than the Mayor King.
They intimidate people to bow down and kiss their rings."
    "Kid, the Godheads are old but with age comes wisdom.
You can either take your chances outside or sit and listen.
This damned, forsaken anti-Godhead society we're in
have left folks void of faith and lost from within.
Things may seem grim but take it from me:

The Godheads aren't trying any form trickery.
"Then why have they blinded us from their light?
We're bastards and heathens cast from their sight.
They starve our bellies while they're plump with pleasures,
living high on a hog while we writhe in their leftovers.
Besides, who should listen to the outdated tales
from a tongue that whiskey has long ago staled?"
    Giving up, Nick rose his flask to take a sip
but instead let a story spill from his lips:
    "Nobody takes me seriously these days.
They think I'm a fool, some vagrant craze.
At one point in Time, I was respected,
a person of repute, but then I was rejected."
    Continuing on, Nick explained his tale,
a time long before his love for whiskey and ale:
    Old Nick Knave had a misnomer surname,
as he was more honest than anybody came.
His moral compass could locate true north,
and lead those who sought it towards its proper course.
In a long ago time Nick used to make toys
for kids with no means to acquire those joys.
After a while, their greed and ungratefulness
became prevalent, and Nick started giving out less.
The children and parents all cursed him with shuns,
then gave him the name he is currently dubbed.
Growing bitter with them, Nick closed up his shop,
then moved to new locations taking other jobs.
But his name followed him wherever he stopped,
so he turned to drinking while he freelanced his lot.
Eventually, he ended up mining for gold,
but lately, all he was able to find was coal.
    Mr. Poochikins asked why Nick had not changed
his name to one of more favorable acclaim.
Nick fell quiet, stepped back into his brain,
let out a long sigh, then began to explain:

"What is the point of hiding scars
when the ones who inflicted them know where they are?
Every relationship should be circular."
He said as he drew one out in the air.
"Without reciprocation, it's all for naught,
and someone usually ends up distraught.
The world turned its back on me, and so I
turned a one-eighty to complete the goodbye.
I don't need people to tell me who I am.
I wish I would have known this before the drinking began.
Don't let a society control your decisions.
Being true to one's self is worth the rejection.
A penny is more precious in the palm of a pauper
than a pile of gold to one that is prospered.
Stop worrying about what you're without.
and cherish the things that you have now."
  With that perspective, Mr. Poochikins' pondered,
allowing his thoughts to purposefully wander.
Was he living his life the way he wanted to?
Or living it out the way he was taught to?
The happiness that he thought would come
was now more lost than he had become.
  Mr. Poochikins decided to remove all the prosthetics,
but bolts and welds kept the detachment prevented.
He would have to wait for the pale morning Glow
of the Monolith to shine before he would go
back to the doctor's and remove the devices.
But for now, Mr. Poochikins would take Nick's advice.
  Speechless, the two sat and reflected
getting lost in the past inside their own heads.
Then Mr. Poochikins noticed the ticking and tocks
of all of Nick Knave's illegal clocks.
Then he asked him, curiosity piqued,
  "Why do you need more than one timepiece?"
Didn't the Mayor King order them banned?

Aren't you afraid of going against his command?
"They symbolize when the Godheads rebelled
against Chaos and when Order was assembled.
That is not something that should be trashed,
so the Mayor King can eat my freckled black ass.
Without me, there would be no coal.
Then the Monolith would soon lose the Glow."
 They both sat in silence, looking at each other,
until Nick broke out with uproarious laughter.
Mr. Poochikins shook his head for a while,
and for the first time Mr. Poochikins smiled.

End Canto 2

70

Canto 3:
Mr. Poochikins' Temper

    In the small hour lights of the Iron Horse cabin,
Nick Knave and Mr. Poochikins continued their conversation.
The two looked at the time the clock faces told
just as the Monolith shined with it's Glow.
Looking at each other they said their goodbyes,
then Mr. Poochikins left with his spirits held high.
    Traversing back to the good doctor's place,
Mr. Poochikins heard sounds so remarkably strange:
Faint scrapings like dragging lead pipes on cement,
and clank-clangings of mechanized instruments.
Hisses and whirs resonated an ambience
of a dirge-like soundtrack throughout the Chrysalis.
The Wight were about walking dressed up full-clad
in devices like ones Mr. Poochikins had.
Decked out from end to end, down to their cores,
with makeshift metals from their backs to their fores.
As strange as it seemed, and so sad to take in,
the Wight appeared to emulate Mr. Poochikins:
Bandaging small abnormalities due to insecurities
unique to their own individual idiosyncrasies.
    Havoc had broken out with riots and violence.
Fires ignited with molotov mindlessness.
As conflicts crawled all over, crowding the streets,
the Wight behaved like brawling dim-witted beasts.

Most fights were over prosthetic attire—
who wore it best or whose stilts were higher.
Some wore fake feet because their step lost its hitch,
and ocular implants just to tame an eye-twitch.
One short and stout Wight walked with the height of a building,
well over 10-stories, like an arachnid scaffolding.
But their limbs got tied up and strangled themselves,
then collapsed like a house imploding in on itself.
They stumbled and tumbled till they fatally fell,
ringing their bell with a skull cracking death knell.
They writhed around like making a snow angel,
but made up of blood and bent skeletal metal.
    In a quest to perfect their outwardly flaws
the Wight found only reasons to hate what they saw.
They weren't trying to better or help themselves,
but rather display their fashion and wealth.
A feeling passed through Mr. Poochikins,
one that pitied the Wight, felt sorrow for the them.
So he left them to their devices and needs,
he knew now that they would never see how he sees.
Though no longer banal and no longer plain,
yet in the end the Wight were still all the same.
    The lights were off of Dr. Good's marquee.
It was mute with its talk but still grinning eerily.
He knocked at the door, no one answered his rap.
He pushed on the door and found no locks were latched.
As it yawned open that same foul smell rushed by
like a frantic mob of shoppers in search of a buy.
After announcing his presence he took a step deeper,
but his efforts did not bring out the shop's keeper.
So into that black void of nothing he walked,
but just as he entered his leg's engine stopped.
After several attempts to turn over the motor,
he tried to remove it, but couldn't budge the enclosure.

His limp was worse now more than ever,
as he struggled to drag his leg across the floor.

Other than him the place was quiet, but not quite silent:
Behind a closed door that was marked private
came a staticky shrill, like a wheel of pins
being drug across strings of a tin violin.
A contrast of colors refusing to blend
flashed through the jambs so he pushed the door open.
A silhouette sat before strange machines
and a honeycombed wall of lighted up screens.

Each flickering cell televised pictures
depicting the violence the Wight did to each other.
The doctor sat before the screens, completely transfixed,
while he thumbed buttons and toyed with joysticks,
not noticing someone was standing behind him,
watching and listening to the soliloquies he recited:

"With a pocket full of poesies and a fist of pantomimes,
with the sleight of hand I manipulate your lives.

With ropes around your wrists I bend you to my whims,
dance you 'round like marionettes, strung up by the limbs.
Like needlework I sow a set sutures to your sins,
but I reap with every stitch, you're all cushions for my pins."
    Mr. Poochikins' head cocked like a curious dog
letting the gears of his thoughts take root into cogs:
What is he doing? Is he controlling the Wight?
Is he the cause of all the madness outside!
Mr. Poochikins gasped in shock which caught
the doctor's attention, who then sparked up the sweet talk.
    "Mr. Poochikins, why are you aliv… I mean… here?
Shouldn't you be somewhere other than… here?"
    The doctor's smile still stretched from ear to ear
but his convincing words no longer appeared.
Though still so naive, Mr. Poochikins knew
that something was amiss, but the doctor continued:
    "Please, Mr. Poochikins, don't misunderstand.
What you're seeing here is not the work of my hands."
    Dr. Good showed his palms, Mr. Poochikins looked,
then the doctor struck him down with a vicious left hook.
    Making for the exit, the doctor ran away,
while Mr. Poochikins laid on the ground and splayed.
He grabbed the first thing he found off the floor,
aimed, then threw it straight toward the door.
Just as the doctor tried to finish his escape
the barber pole struck him in the back of his legs.
After the pole hit its mark, it rolled around
to the base of the chair, while the doctor fell down,
knocking over the shelves of inky fluid,
shattering jars, making the air quite polluted.
    The doctor splish-splashed in the black aftermath,
as he crawled through sharp shards of broken glass.
His palms split open, blood gushed from the skin,
then his cuts burned as the aether mixed in.
In an attempt to get up he made his way to the chair,

but before he could stand Mr. Poochikins stood there.
He shoved Doctor Good down into the seat,
then with his crutch, bludgeoned both of his knees.
    "That will keep you from running away again."
Mr. Poochikins said to the knee-capped man.
    Writhing in pain, folding over the chair,
the doctor stared straight in the pool of black aether.
Hung up he waited for Hindsight's projection
but his search did not cast any type of reflection.
    "How I hate irony," the doctor said to the floor,
"AND you're a bit more strong-willed than I hoped for."
    Mr. Poochikins advanced and expressed to the doctor,
before confessing to him something a bit awkward:
    "I want you to remove these machinations.
Take off these contradicting contraptions.
I changed myself for all the wrong reasons.
I see nothing in error of me, outside or in."
    Then Doctor Good said with a mocking guffaw.
"Good luck with that. They've been all Crafted on."
    "I don't care how you put 'em on, just take them off!"
Mr. Poochikins yelled, which echoed through the shop.
    "You wouldn't know, would you? Because…
you're not like how I am and how my mother… was."
    The stretched out smile on the doctor's face seemed
less of a mile now and more like a yard reaped.
He sucked up the emotions that welled in his eyes,
and expelled to Mr. Poochikins the thoughts on his mind:
"In order to Craft, one must sacrifice,
and the cost is always a physical price.
I Crafted your machinations from my own brain,
and each piece acts like a link in a chain.
By mellon-balling all the sadness from my mind,
I manipulated all the Wights' and your lives.
So it's impossible for Crafts to be withdrawn,
not unless you kill the one who put them on.

So kill me now, Mr. innocent Poochikins.
Kill me and see who you truly are within."
    The doctor continued to talk as he sat back in the seat,
holding his hands up again this time in defeat.
    "You're more familiar with Crafting than you know.
Remember that large candy cane that you stole?
That thing you took was the Coma Candy Cane.
I knew you ate it when I saw your tooth decay.
The cane is meant to put those who eat it asleep,
so their bodies can be harvested for the Mayor King's needs.
Its Crafted from the blood of little children,
and my mother intended for it to herd more of them."
    Mr. Poochikins said nothing to the broken legged man,
he only limped around while his thoughts again ran:
Who is this doctor? What is going on?
Where did he come from? When did I go wrong?
How did he do all of this? Why is it happening?
His lack of answers became horribly maddening.
Then he stopped limping around, pacing for a clue,
before finally asking the doctor, "Who are you?"
    "My mother taught me a great deal of skills,
from mechanics and clockwork, to the Crafting of spells.
I used them in the trade of tricks and deceit,
and how to enslave the feeble minded and weak."
    The doctor said, as he pulled out a bag,
whose contents clamored with a marbly clang.
He threw the parcel towards Mr. Poochikins,
who spilled out the contents of what was within.
A pair of eyes fell out of the mass
into his palm, which were encased in glass.
They both glared at him with a purposeful stare,
and their color stood up the back of his hairs:
They were red, a red that blinded his sight.
They were the Hag's from pupils to whites.
Then a thought slacked his jaw, for a second he paused,

and all became clear the pain the doctor had caused.
   "You're mother? The Hag was your moth…?"
   "YES!" The doctor interrupted and affirmed.
"The old woman you murdered without remorse,
by shoving in front of the Iron Horse,
was my dear old mother, the Red Eyed Hag,
you fuck, and you'll pay and bleed till you beg.
She'd still be alive had you not walked by.
And the Wight just stood there and watched as she died."
   Mr. Poochikins felt no regret for what he'd done.
Nothing inspired repentance in him, none.
But a burden did weigh down upon his brow:
How long he let her and the Wight beat him down.
The past and the beatings could not be forgiven,
and his violence was the product of that situation.
   Dr. Good filled the air back up with his talk
while Mr. Poochikins remained with his thoughts.
   "You know what's comical about this theatrical set?
Life is a pending tragedy; it always ends in death.
After she died, sadness seeded the furrows
of my face and from them grew a great sorrow.
So I carved off its skin from temple to temple,
and made masks that suited those two theatrical symbols.
Do you see now, my dear Mr. Poochikins?
Now only I chose when to frown or to grin."
   The look on Mr. Poochikins' face was almost vacant,
but he was there behind wide eyes of amazement.
A slight shake of his head acknowledged disbelief,
as awkward laughter accepted the doctor's stage of grief.
   "Yeah, life is pretty funny, that much I can relate.
I never knew such a beast of a bitch could procreate.
I see now you have more than your mother's eyes.
You're just as bat-shit as she was before she died.
You play puppeteer, attaching strings to promises,
sowing those broken with lies and quick fixes.

You preach nurseries to convert the weak and ill,
manipulate the disadvantaged, come in for the kill,
then pull back the lines and reel them in
for another chance to subdue them again.
You're dishonest and corrupted…"
    "OH! *Whine! Whine!* " the doctor again interrupted.
"Shut up! You whinny, hypocritical freak.
You're words reek high of low and base deeds,
So drop the sob-song, Mr. Puppetkins.
You perpetuated the hell that you're in
by keeping yourself under the turn of a key,
and staying locked up in your self-made misery.
I might wear these theatrical and false faces,
but its you who masks their true appearances.
Stop pretending you're a good person.
You don't care how I've treated them.
And you would know the pain of a son's loss
had you a parent to weigh up the cost."
    Mr. Poochikins knew what the doctor said was true,
but he continued to defend his own point of view:
    "The Wight are impressionable, they know not what they do.
But now with the Hag completely removed,
in time, they'll adapt and find ways that are new.
They may even embrace me as brother, too.
I'm not like you and I'm not like the Wight.
I'm better than you, at least in my sight.
Just because they would do that to me
doesn't mean that's how I need to be."
    The doctor chimed in with an acerbic segue:
    "What? Is your tongue as deformed as your leg?
Are you void of reason, or plagued with Tourette's?
That self-righteous garbage you're spitting out's useless.
Before you point your finger, you'd lick it clean,
because it's filthy and stained with a bloody gleam.
A sin is a sin, my dear Mr. Poochikins,

and you are a product of your very own kin."
    Mr. Poochikins agreed with that last statement,
but felt his kith's actions were from social enslavement.
So he paced back and forth with his limp heavy limb,
getting lost in his thought for the second time again.
But he thought for too long and lost track of Time's flow
so the doctor bashed his head striped with the barber's pole.
And when this happened a reaction took place,
one that kept the doctor from making an escape.
    Mr. Poochikins' anger soon boiled to rage,
roiling it down till only violence remained.
Synapses started to short in his brain,
and his calmed face began to reanimate.
Sparks cascaded from his mercurial eye,
like an abrasive wheel working away at a grind.
His mind was a battlefield. His brain was under war.
He started having trouble holding up his frontal fore.
His flesh bubbled up like boiling wax
with boils and blisters as his body gained mass.
The growth stretched his skin, broadening bones.
He cried out in anguish with a blood curdling bellow.
His muscle expansion left him malformed,
leaving every part of him grossly deformed.
Each part of his body swelled 5-times in size
but one arm was triple the size of the 5-times.
The weight of it which then hunched him over
revealing the mountains that became his shoulders.
His left leg remained much more longer in length
than the other but both were equally of the same strength.
Clutching the grid of metal that lined his mouth,
he tore off the device that kept his head bound.
Its braces came off with a series of snaps,
popping like nitroglycerin filled bubble wrap.
Jagged teeth jutted, no longer like bone,
but rather resembling knapped out flint stone.

Mr. Poochikins changed into a creature of horror,
a terrible being whose blood thirst never ceased.
Those who have witnesses this creature therefore
have come to call it the Gigascine Beast.

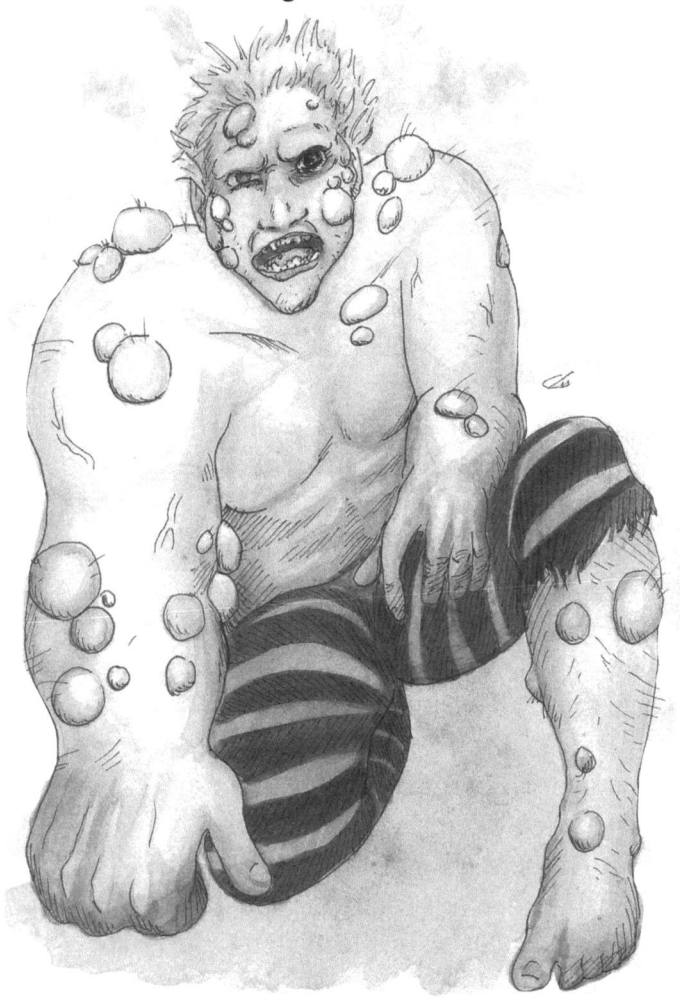

The straps of his forearm crutch had severed and snapped,
so the Beast hurled away causing the ceiling to collapse.
It rapidly soared as it cut through sky
before stopping and lodging into the Monolith's side.
A crack bisected its flawless facade,
but the Monolith still stood, just horribly flawed.

When the Beast grew, it broke the prosthetic on its leg,
releasing the hamsters that had been caged.
When they escaped, they raced and ferally ran,
lunged at the doctor's head then soon began
to doll up his face with tiny incisions,
fleshing out bows as they slashed it ribbons.
That too perfect smile was misplaced from his face,
then they scratched out his eyes with curt, vengeful haste.
By tooth and nail they gnawed and they clawed
until Dr. Good could see nothing at all.
As he writhed and screamed, he swatted frantically
at the volatile critters before they ran away free.
   "You ungrateful rodents," the doctor harshly squawked,
"are in severe need of more cattle prod shocks.
And you, my little, bad Mr. Puppykins
are a rabid mutt in need of a mercy-injection.
You truly are an abomination.
a bastard child unfit for this civilization."
   The Gigascine Beast did not speak a peep,
it only communicated by the breathes it heaved.
The Beast's sight went to red, then changed to rage-black.
Its temper rose up tracking a vehement path.
Having enough, the behemoth palmed the chair,
ripped and raised it from its mount to the air
then struck it down on Dr. Good's skull,
shattering the bones like a breaking glass bulb.
Each leg of the doctor's sprang up and kicked.
His right eye convulsed, while the left stayed static.
His lips quivered slightly, clenched up then locked,
vacantly staring at the man he had mocked.
The good doctor felt his stomach tighten and wrench.
He vomited blood as his teeth slowly clenched.
As his thoughts cut to black, he rolled back his eyes.
As Time slipped away, blindly he died.

Peering into the doctor's caved in cranium,
the Gigascine Beast saw the bright shine of chrome.
The jagged concave of his skull revealed
not just brains but winding gears and cogwheels.

The dead body sat there, head broken open,
posed like a child's toy, alone and forgotten,
lying akimbo, limbs completely offset.
A motionless minikin. A lifeless puppet.
Like a slow skipping track on a broken record,
the doctor lifelessly repeated two words:
    "Puppetkins. Mr. Puppetkins. Puppetkins…"
On and on. Even in death the madman mocked him.
    Comedic. Tragic. Death. Thought the Gigascine Beast,
as his shadow towered over the recently deceased.

Its rage then lead it to the doctor's back room,
and smashed the devices that kept the Wight's mind consumed.
The fallen screens sparked with a staticky flicker
and into the welcoming arms of the aether.
A fire spread like a smile as it started to crack,
cackling wildly into a maniacal laugh.
  The Beast bored out the shop and into the streets
with destruction following the wake of its feet.
Outside the shop and inside the night,
as the inferno raged on, so did the Wight.
Still combating themselves as the shop-fire grew.
Even engulfed in flames, their fighting continued.
Seeing this madness, the Beast felt compelled
to help them escape from this living hell.
But all of its efforts were completely in vein
as the doctor's devices had changed their brains.
The Beast gave up efforts to free all of them,
and decided to save itself from the mayhem.
  The Gigascine Beast climbed hand over hand,
scaling the Chrysalis of Concrete and Tin.
Taking the fall down into the waste-water moat,
the Beast swam through the bodily fluids it bestowed.
It rowed through sewage the Chrysalis coughed up
until the Beast met the end, covered in black muck.
  Morphing back into a less morbid level,
Mr. Poochikins felt more himself and less so a devil.
His clothes were sludgy, tattered asunder.
As he gathered himself, his attention wandered
to the blaze that bit wildly away at the darkness,
brightly dinning upon all of the Chrysalis.
  As flames tongued the sky, one piece of him grew
while the rest inside him was slowly consumed.
Even though his life there had been bad,
a trail of regret mixed with the blood on his hands.

As his once home slipped into blankets of flames,
the screams of the Wight burning alive soon waned.
Then he heard the whistle of the Iron Horse train
and saw it moving down into the sub-terrain.
Nick had survived, but could only hide
down below in caverns where coal was inside.
The doctor was right, he was a beast.
And like the Wight thought, he was a freak.
    The Monolith still stood though scathed from the flames.
And the crack from his crutch stuck out like a vein.
The Mayor King had most likely survived,
and would hunt him down whether dead or alive.
    Lost, paradoxically homesick, tongue-tied with thoughts,
he bit down this self-yarning and swallowed the knot
of strain down his throat to digest the pain
of knowing there was no returning again.
He reversed his gaze, let his back say goodbye,
then walked toward the Forest Melina's tree line.
    Around and before him lay a vast and dark mass—
black trees so tall they cut out the horizon's expanse.

End Canto 3

84

Bios

Courtney

Courtney Pokela is a visual artist who uses a variety of mediums and methods to design, illustrate, and create. Having lived in rural Minnesota her whole life, she often gravitates towards nature as inspiration. Effort is placed in her creations to balance macabre or unassuming themes with charming and engaging elements.

Since she was a child Courtney has been drawing, working with clay, and creating. In her adult life she has completed a range of art commissions and several art show pieces. Courtney has had two years of formal art training and many hours practicing and building on techniques independently.

Courtney practices sculpture, assemblage, drawing, painting, illustration, and the preservation of bones, insects, and plants. She incorporates a variety of mixed media and textiles into her works including organic components. In addition to assembled creations, Courtney uses ink, watercolor, acrylic paints, pastels, and pencil.

Jak

Jacqueline "Jak" Nealy, is a Minnesotan tattoo artist, originally hailing from Bristol, England. A proud dog mother of 3, she lives in the Twin Cities area where she owns and manages two tattoo shops—Twisted Image Tattoo and Iron Rhino Tattoo.

In her late teens, Jak received her first tattoo. Then thinking that she could do a better job than her tattooer, she began her career in the industry during the 1990s.

Since then, her reputation has lead her to being about to tattoo some of the members from Minnesota band American Head Charge.

Additionally, she has a affinity towards pirates, and proudly waves the Jolly Roger with her middle finger on the trigger of a rebel life.

Lyssa

Lyssa Greywood has a in BA in Creative Writing with Honors, and an MA in Transliteration and Screenwriting. She is from Europe and has a passion about storytelling with an expertise in a variety of topics.

She covers subjects anywhere from care and history of domestic breeds, health, home improvement, and travel. She is experienced with online content such blog writing, SEO, and digital copywriting.

She also teaches and develops learning guides for students.

August Daft

He dibbles and dabbles with scribbles, but not Scrabble, all the while holding a handful of grey scaled Skittles. He has no real accolades, preferring to flex his literary ego like a teenage boy curling his gangly muscles in front of a mirror.

Originally from rural Minnesota, in a town place just south of hell, but lives in Greater Minnesota by heart.

He prefers the company of woman to a fault.

You will often see his hands stained with ink because his a sloppy writer. He likes to eat dosa scomps with Roy G. Biv.

If you really want to drown to death in someone else's ego, find August. He will talk you all the way down into the depressing abyss that is his soul.